T0326035

Kofi

GROWING PAINS

H L DANIEL

Kofi

GROWING PAINS

H L DANIEL

MEREO
Cirencester

Mereo Books

1A The Wool Market Dyer Street Cirencester Gloucestershire GL7 2PR
An imprint of Memoirs Publishing www.mereobooks.com

Kofi - Growing Pains: 978-1-86151-433-2

First published in Great Britain in 2015
by Mereo Books, an imprint of Memoirs Publishing

The address for Memoirs Publishing Group Limited can be found at
www.memoirspublishing.com

The Memoirs Publishing Group Ltd Reg. No. 7834348

The Memoirs Publishing Group supports both The Forest Stewardship Council® (FSC®) and the
PEFC® leading international forest-certification organisations. Our books carrying both the FSC
label and the PEFC® and are printed on FSC®-certified paper. FSC® is the only
forest-certification scheme supported by the leading environmental organisations including
Greenpeace. Our paper procurement policy can be found at
www.memoirspublishing.com/environment

Typeset in 12/18pt Bembo
by Wiltshire Associates Publisher Services Ltd. Printed and bound in Great Britain
by Printondemand-Worldwide, Peterborough PE2 6XD

Dedicated to my father

S. I. Iddrissu

The sunrise continues to radiate your smile!

Chapter One

I rise with the sound of the talking drums. As the unspoken words echo through the thin walls of my bedroom, I feel my spirit soar. I know the meaning of every beat and rhythm. Papa taught me. As his first son, he expects me to grow into an intelligent, courageous and responsible man. 'A man who can step into his shoes', he says, 'when the time comes'. He says a man who doesn't know where he comes from is like a tree without roots or branches.

To prevent me from becoming a stick, he began teaching me, from the moment I could speak, about my ancestors, custom, tradition and culture. Papa brought me up with the fear of God and respect for my elders. By the time I was ten I had read the Bible and knew nearly every psalm, hymn and proverb. What he can't stand is people who travel abroad for a few years and come back acting as if they have forgotten their mother tongues, speak with foreign accents, only eat foreign foods and behave like foreigners. I guess he wants to ensure that I don't get lost and confused.

He needn't worry, because I don't want to live abroad. I love living in Techiman, the legendary birthplace of the Akan people. It is one of the two main towns in Brong Ahafo, the other being the regional capital, Sunyani. Bordered to the north by the Black Volta River, to the east by Lake Volta, to the south by the Ashanti, Eastern and Western regions, and to the west by Ivory Coast, Brong Ahafo is one of the most attractive regions in Ghana. It produces most of the country's cocoa and agriculture.

My home was built over fifty years ago by my great-grandfather. It is a large round structure consisting of ten separate huts, built with red clay, straw and wood. The natural products make it free from harmful toxins and friendly to the environment. And the exterior surfaces are grooved so that when it rains the water can drain away easily.

I come from a family of cocoa farmers. My great-grandfather, grandfather, father and uncles are all cocoa farmers. I do enjoy working on the farm with Papa, my uncles and cousins. Most of the time I prune the trees and clear the weeds and when the crops are harvested I help to cut the pods and to ferment and dry the cocoa beans. When fermented and processed, the rich aroma of the cocoa bean produces one of the most sought-after and desired flavours in the world - chocolate. It's great to know that by farming and the exporting cocoa my family helps with the growth of the country's economy.

Chocolate has many health benefits. It reduces depression, produces feel-good chemicals in the brain, protects our cells from destruction and reduces the risk of diseases. The cocoa bean has protective antioxidants, which keep our heart and blood vessels healthy. Carl Linnaeus, the Swedish natural scientist, gave cocoa a most appropriate botanical name, *Theobroma*, which means 'food of the gods'. I love the food of the gods, from the sweet pulp of the ripened pod to everything made from chocolate - bars with toffee, caramel, nuts and raisins, biscuits, cakes, and hot drinks; cocoa, milo, Ovaltine. Maame only buys them on special occasions, but that is OK with me because I like to stay slim and don't ever want to visit the dentist. Left to themselves, my sisters Adwoa and Akua and my brothers Kojo and Kwaku would eat chocolate every day.

Sometimes I wonder how things might have turned out if Tetteh Quarshie hadn't brought cocoa seedlings from the island of Fernando Po in the Gulf of Guinea to Ghana, formerly known as Gold Coast. It was the very first seeds that he planted at Mampong in1879 that led to the country's success in the cocoa industry and has made Ghana one of the largest cocoa-producing countries in the world.

Chapter Two

I have been up for ages, yet it still looks dark outside. As the sound of the drums get fainter and fainter, I roll over onto my side and turn up the light on the lantern.

I haven't told Papa that I want to become a doctor. It will break his heart, because he expects me to be a farmer. It's not that I don't want to, but ever since I was a child, I have watched my grandpa Suleman, a traditional healer, use herbal medicines to cure a wide variety of ailments. Seeing the joy on the faces of the people he heals and their families makes me want to be just like him. He also happens to be the kindest person I know, and he never takes money from the people he heals. He will give his last penny and the clothes off his back to those who need it more than him, and invites hungry people off the street to share his food. I think God blessed him with the gift of healing because of his good deeds.

I call my mother Maame, but her name is Yaa Amponsah. She knows that it's my dream to make sick people better, just like her father. She says that even though I don't have Grandpa's special gift, I can be anything I choose to be if I work hard at it.

When I told my teacher that I wanted to be a doctor, he said I could do it, if I did very well in every subject, especially maths and science. So I studied very hard, was punctual at school, never missed a lesson, paid attention in class, answered questions and did all my homework in time. Some of my friends and schoolmates called me a bookworm, but I wasn't bothered. What got me is that even with all my efforts, I never came first in class. It was as if that position was always reserved for the same people; Lydia, Iddrissu, Daniel and Zhara. They topped the class every year.

Maame says she is proud of me for gaining Bs and Cs in all my subjects. When she found me in my room, worrying about the common entrance exams, she said, 'Kofi, you've done everything you can possibly do. I am sure that with your efforts and my prayers, you will succeed. The Almighty has a plan for each and every one of us. Look at my fingers.' I looked at the long slim fingers with dark brown nail polish.' Are they equal?'

I shook my head.

'Exactly!' she responded, with that special smile of hers. 'What matters is that you do your best. And if you don't succeed at the first hurdle, just dust yourself off and keep trying. The race is not for the swiftest, but those who will win, and I have no doubt that you will be a winner, so stop fretting and go out and play. What will be will be!'

She was right about me being a winner. When the results came I couldn't believe it. I got top marks and was offered a place at my first choice secondary school, Achimota. That day I screamed so much I lost my voice.

When Papa heard the news, he beat his chest with pride. Now he walks with a spring in his step and his chest purposely puffed out. Maame gave thanks to God for answering her prayers, then she ran around and told everyone in our compound and ran to her father's compound and told everyone there.

I can't wait to start college. There have been lots of stories about the capital city, Accra. They say it is very modern with huge houses, posh cars, fine women, clubs, restaurants and lots of things to do. Some even brag about their wild experiences there. I don't want to do anything wild or bad, but it would be nice to see it for myself.

There have been whispers throughout town that I will

be leaving for the big city in a few days. It has turned me into an overnight celebrity. People who had never said a word to me are now bending over backwards to get to know me. The area champions who looked me up and down and kissed their teeth just for looking at them are all over me like a rash. But I don't want girls like them, walking around with their knickers showing. And when they are told to cover up they say 'I am aware!' Noooo, I want a good girl from a good home, not ones who will eat me alive!

Chapter Three

The rising sun greets me as I emerge from my hut. A warm breeze blows over my face and bare arms. The birds are chirping in the trees. I spot Torpedo, the two-year-old Alsatian, sprawled under the guava tree in the middle of the compound. He jumps up and sprints towards me. I stroke his thick golden coat, knowing I will miss him, terribly.

Gazing across the length and breadth of the compound, I notice the wall gecko crawling up the cocoa tree and the chicks nestled under the big brown hen. The hen reminds me of Maame and how protective she is over me. Left to her alone I would remain at home forever. I don't know how I will survive without her delicious fufu and palm-nut soup, and the finger-licking garden-egg stew with Kobe (salt fish) and yam she makes every Sunday.

I know Kwame is up when I hear the sound of feet crushing down on stone.

'Good morning, Kwame.'

'Morin Kofi!' he says, 'You up early. Still tinking 'bout leaving for big city?'

'Yes, how do you know?'

He is standing in front of his hut. A piece of cloth is draped around his waist and a chewing stick lodged firmly between his teeth.

'Is all over you face!' he says. He spits and heads towards the bathroom.

He is right. It's not often that I wake up before sunrise. Kwame is my uncle Ameyaw's son. He is twenty-one and his nickname is Iron Mike. He looks just like Mike Tyson, the boxer - short, sturdy, broad shoulders, deep-set eyes and a massive neck. He enjoys strenuous work like chopping trees, digging and lugging heavy sacks of cocoa from the farm to the market. He says it keeps him strong and maintains his six-pack. Even though he looks fierce, deep down he is a pussycat.

I can hear Maame stirring in her hut. Shortly after I turned thirteen, she decided I could have my own hut and cleared the one next to hers for me. It felt great having all that space to myself. Not that I minded sharing a hut with my brothers - it was fun, most of the time. But now I can hear myself think without any of their pranks.

Everyone keeps telling me I have become a man, but it doesn't mean I can do anything I want. Maame still checks on me, especially when my friends come to visit. She is not keen on female visitors either. With her eagle eyes, ears that hear everything and instincts stronger than a detective, I wouldn't dare invite a girl over. I wouldn't put it past her to shoo them out for fear of corrupting me. What she doesn't know is that the women who come to her stall are worse than the girls at my school.

Chapter Four

As it is Saturday, we need to get to the market very early. By six o'clock I have brushed my teeth and showered and am ready for breakfast. My *obronyi-waawu* jeans are faded and ripped at the knees; I think it looks trendy, like what the models wear on the catwalk. My white T-shirt, G–Unit sneakers and Rotary watch are presents from Tamara. She is a family friend and Maame's favourite customer.

The aroma of sweetbread and omelette whets my appetite. Maame is still getting ready, so I join my brothers, sisters and cousins under the guava tree for breakfast.

'Good morning, Maame,' I say when she finally

emerges. She loves to take her time when dressing and she always looks beautiful.

'Good morning, my son,' she says tying a piece of the stylish green cloth around her tiny waist. Her hair is worn in fine braids and falls just below her neck. I take the heavy bag from her while she hugs my brothers and sisters and gives them chores to do.

As we make our way down the hill, traders loading foodstuffs on lorries bound for the market greet us. Everyone stops to greet Maame. She is a pillar of the community and admired for her kindness and compassion, for fighting for what she believes in and for her business skills.

Thick air rushes through the marketplace, carrying dust and the smell of fumes from lorries and trucks as we approach it. There is loud music all around us. People are speaking at the top of their voices in Dagbani, Hausa, Ewe, Ga, Fante, Twi and English. The market is nearly always busy, but even more so on Saturdays when traders from neighbouring villages display their pottery, woven fabrics, beads and carvings to attract tourists from the Kintampo Waterfalls, Bosomoa Forest Reserve, Pumpum River and the Boabeng Fiema Monkey Sanctuary.

Our shop is in the quieter part of the market. We sell sacks of cocoa beans. The male customers tend to know exactly what they want. They come in, choose the products, pay and go. The female customers like to take their time. After enquiring how Maame is, they go on and on about what they have been up to, and move on to me. 'Your son is handsome, ooh!' they say, or 'I can't believe it! Kofi has turned into a fine young man,' or, 'Your son is such a hunk. If only I were a few years younger,' and 'If I were you, I would watch out for the sugar mummies before they pounce on your son!'

Maame doesn't know that they have already started. Ever since I turned thirteen I've been noticing a lot of things that I hadn't thought of before. I may be nearly six feet tall, but I am still a teenager.

One of her customers is a very rich lady in her fifties. Whenever she comes to the shop she will ask if I can carry her bags to her car. She likes to give me big tips, but she also likes touching me. I always run back to the shop when she starts. Being alone with her gives me the creeps. The other day she invited me over to her house for dinner. I turned her down, of course. Do I look like I am starving?

There is another lady who comes to the shop, Tamara. Just as I am thinking about her, she walks into the shop. I can hear my heart beating. She is in her twenties, very pretty, and she wears the nicest clothes.

'Tammy!' Maame says with a huge smile.

She rushes over in a figure hugging dress and very high heels and gives Maame a hug. 'Yaa Amponsah, so good to see you. How have you been?'

'Busy, but fine. You look beautiful. When did you return from New York?'

'Yesterday. Is my order ready?'

'Yes. Kwame has delivered it to the shippers.'

'Thank you so much.' She turns to me with gorgeous green eyes and smiles. My heart stops beating.

'Kofi, how are you?'

'I am fine' I respond and look away. She makes me feel things that I know I shouldn't.

She says something to Maame, stops mid-sentence and glances at me.

'Kofi, I hear you are off to college, so I got you a few things from New York. They are the latest fashion, you will love them! Oh, I nearly forgot...' She pulls out a white envelope from her bag and gives it to me.

'Thank you' I say grim-faced.

'Why don't you open it?' Tamara asks keenly.

Maame is staring at me, so I open the envelope. It is full of brand new fifty cedi notes. I hand it to Maame and walk away.

'Kofi, come back here!' Maame yells. 'Why the long face?'

I move slowly towards them, eyes looking down.

Maame gives me one of her looks. 'What is wrong with you? Where are your manners?'

'Thank you Aunty Tamara,' I say quickly, forcing a smile.

'It is my pleasure, Dear. Come with me. Your things are in the boot.' She gives Maame a hug. 'Yaa Amponsah I need to run now. Thank you again, for everything.'

I follow Tamara. When we reach the car park she clicks the alarm. The back lights of a brand new black Mercedes SLK start flashing. She opens the boot, grabs a brown Louis Vuitton bag and hands it to me. Then, just as I turn to leave, she grabs my hand. She is so close I can smell her perfume.

'Kofi, are you OK?'

I nod.

She throws back her long black hair and puts an arm around me. 'Have I done anything to upset you?' Her voice is soft and warm.

I feel a lump in my throat. 'No. It's just that I've got a lot on my mind.'

'Good.' She licks her pink glossy lips. 'Can I take you out to lunch, before you leave for college?'

I stratch my head. 'Ehmmm, I will be going to the farm with Papa. Every day before I leave.'

'Don't worry' she says. 'Why don't you open the bag?'

Even though she is smiling, I can tell she is disappointed. I open the bag and look inside. Jeans, shirts, shorts, T-shirts, trainers, socks and another watch.

'Thank you,' I say politely and close the bag.

'I am glad you like them. You better get back before your mother starts worrying.'

As I turn to leave, she kisses me. The feel of her soft lips on my cheek makes me feel funny all over. My hands are shaking so much, I drop the bag. I pick it up and walk quickly to the shop, without a backward glance. I feel very hot and start to sweat.

Maame is serving a male customer. I breath a sigh of relief, and greet him. Then I grab a can of coke from the fridge, hop on the counter and turn on the radio. Michael Jackson is singing *Off The Wall*. It reminds me to brush up my moonwalk skills. I check the time. It's not even noon yet. I can't wait to go home and play football with my brothers.

Learning about puberty and reproduction at school has helped me understand some of the things that have been happening to me. Like how I felt when Tamara kissed me. Over the past year my body has changed so much, and sometimes it seems to have a mind of its own. My hormones seem to be going crazy, like they've been hibernating under my skin all these years and can't wait to break free. I seem to be growing taller each day, my head is getting bigger, my nose looks wide, my hands are getting large and my fingers look longer. Maame had to buy me new shoes because my feet have jumped from a size six to a nine. My arms and legs have stretched so much that my torso and shoulders are struggling to catch up with the rest of my body. I am beginning to feel like a freak, with all the pubic hairs, hairs in my armpit, some popping out of the corners of my upper lip and spreading to my top lip, below my bottom lip, the corners of my cheek, the sides of my face, my chin and places I didn't know hair grew from. The other day I had to look in the mirror so I could be sure the voice coming out of my mouth was my own. And now my face is under attack from spots and zits.

Sometimes I wonder why anyone would find me attractive. Maybe this thing about Tamara is a figment of my imagination. How can a beautiful, elegant lady who can have any man she wants be interested in a pimple-faced, lanky teenager like me?

Chapter Five

It's the third of September 2004, the day before I leave for college. My school clothes and everything required in the prospectus are packed in my trunk. Maame has loaded my chop box with provisions - cans of milk, sugar, cornflakes, sardines, corned beef, milo, Ovaltine, biscuits, condensed milk toffee and chocolate. Even though she acts like she is OK with me leaving, I know she is tearing up inside. If it were left to her, I would remain at home forever.

I am returning home from the farm with Papa and Torpedo. It's a few minutes past four in the afternoon. Just as we turn the corner I hear music. I am surprised that it's coming from my compound, plus it's my favourite singer, Michael Jackson, so I turn to Papa.

'Is someone having a party at our home?'

His throws his cloth over his shoulders and gives me a broad, toothy grin. 'Mmmmm, let me think...' I hate it when he does that. I can tell he knows what is happening but just wants to keep me in suspense. I wait impatiently as he clears his throat.

'A very clever boy will be leaving home tomorrow. His mother and I decided that since he is not just clever but a very good son whom we love dearly, we should give him a sending-off party.'

At this point I am so excited that I throw down the hoe and cutlass, give him a big hug and race home with Torpedo. The first person I see is Kwame. He is standing next to the ghetto blaster with lots of CDs.

'Kwame!' I say breathlessly 'You should have told me!'

'An' spoir the saprise?' he asks. 'No way! One more saprise for you. Ha ha!'

'Another surprise? Please tell me what it is,' I plead.

'After you wash an' dress very nice.'

'Ahhhhhh!!!!' I scream. He knows I hate surprises.

I find Maame in the kitchen. There is food everywhere; fried rice, yam and palava sauce, cakes, pies, kebabs... Kojo and Kwaku, are busy stuffing their faces. Adwoa and Akua are putting drinks in the fridge. They are all dressed up in party clothes.

'How was your day at the farm?' Maame asks, smiling sweetly.

'Good. Is all this food for my party?'

'Yes, my son. Your party starts in an hour.'

'Maame, tell him to go and have a shower,' says Adwoa. She is such a madam, eleven going on thirty.

'He has mud all over him.' Akua adds. I am not cleaning the kitchen again! And I can smell him from here.' She pulls a face and sticks out her tongue.

'Girls, you better be nice to your big brother,' says Maame, 'or no party food or chocolate for you.'

That gets them on their best behaviour.

On my way out of the kitchen I see my cousins arranging chairs and tables in the garden. They are all dressed in their Sunday best. How come they all know, and I am the last to know about my own party?

Wondering who else has been invited, I grab a bucket and head to the bathroom.

The party is in full swing by six o'clock. Every member of my family is here. Grandpa Suleman and Grandma Dondoful are sitting under the guava tree with my aunts and uncles. I greet each of them. Tamara is chatting to Maame. All my school friends are here, so I go and join them.

I am having a good time with my friends when I notice Samira. She is the best-dressed girl at school. I really like her but I haven't had the courage to speak to her. She is always with her friends. She must be the surprise Kwame was talking about. I had forgotten all about it. I rush over to Kwame. My heart is racing.

'Samira is here! How did she know? Who invited her?'

Kwame smiles cheekily and winks at me. 'Keep coor. I ask her to come.'

'I can't believe she agreed to come.'

'Why not? All the girrs rove you. Many want to come but I invite onry the good ones. I know you rike Samira. I think she rikes you too.'

'OK, thanks, but what do I do? I am confused.'

He grins broadly and whispers 'Take it easy. Go to her, say herro and just tork.' He pats me on the back. 'Go on, make her your girr.'

Taking a deep calming breath, I swagger towards Samira. I wish I was as good with girls as Kwame is. She looks very pretty in a pink lace dress. Her long silky hair is worn in a ponytail. Her face lights up when she sees me. She stops chatting to her friend and looks my way.

'Hi!' I say, 'thanks for coming.'

'Hi!' she responds shyly.

'Can I get you anything?'

'Yes, do you have Fanta?'

'Yes, I think so. Give me a minute.' I have to stop myself from running all the way to the kitchen and back.

Her friend is talking to the other girls, which is great. Just the two of us.

'Here' I say, handing her a bottle of Fanta with a straw.

'Thank you,' she says, and takes it from me. After a while she takes a sip and smiles at me with big brown eyes. I return the smile. How I wish she would be my girl. She is just perfect.

We smile sheepishly at each other until her friend returns. I join my friends, but my eyes remain on Samira. We exchange glances while I am eating, drinking, dancing and doing all the usual teenage stuff.

The grown-ups are a few yards away, seated around the guava tree. The men are sipping palm wine and discussing football matches, while the women share the latest gossip as they nibble on sticks of kebabs. The children are running around, playing hide and seek, and Kwame and his crew are spinning the latest hi-life, hip-hop, soul, jazz and reggae. I am so happy I could burst.

I see my friends off around eight o'clock and walk Samira home. Guided by the moonlight, we listen to the nightingales in the churchyard as we stroll hand in hand in the cool summer breeze.

Samira's lives in a nice part of town, about ten minutes away from my house. Just before we reach her house, a beautiful white two-storey building with a fence and gate, I ask, 'Will you miss me?'

'Of course,' she replies, eyes twinkling like the stars. 'But you can write to me. If you like.'

'Oh yes, I would love that. Can I have your address?'

'It's PO Box 1050.'

'If I write, will you write back?'

'Don't be silly,' she says. 'Why would I ask you to write if I wasn't thinking of writing back?'

'Sorry.' I scratch my head. 'It's just that I hear you girls like to play hard to get.'

'Really?' she pouts. 'Well, I don't! And something else you need to know, I stick to my word. Do you?'

'Absolutely!' I say quickly.

'Good, because I hear you boys like to lie and cheat.'

She may look shy, but she is no pushover. I think she likes me, but I have to be sure.

'Samira, will you be my girlfriend?'

She giggles but doesn't say anything. Her dimples are so cute.

I press on. 'Does that mean you will?'

She smiles and nods.

Her hand is still in mine. I give it a little squeeze. 'Can I kiss you goodbye?'

She looks at me warily. 'OK, but just here.' She points at her cheek.

I give her a quick peck.

She blushes. 'Don't forget to write.' Very slowly she removes her hand from mine and opens the gate.

'Bye, Samira.'

'Bye. PO Box 1050.'

'I won't forget.' I wave. She waves back.

We continue waving at each other until she enters the house and shuts the gate. I am glad she repeated the address. My mind is racing. Ignoring the stirrings within me I head home.

That night, as I toss and turn, all I can think about is Samira. In my dream I kiss her lips, not her cheek, and it feels so good.

Suddenly I wake up. I feel awkward and hug myself until I fall asleep. The next morning I notice the stain on my boxers. Now I know why they call it a wet dream. Jumping out of bed, I hurry to the bathroom for a long cold shower.

Chapter Six

It had not occurred to me that I was poor until I arrived in Accra. Everything is much bigger and nicer here. There are people of every shade, and some of the buildings are much grander than I imagined.

The lorry dropped Kwame and me at the transport station. From there we took a taxi to Achimota College. After being welcomed by the school prefect, we were shown to my dormitory and given a tour of the campus.

I must have stared at every student as we strolled along the picturesque campus and its wooded countryside-like surroundings. They seemed quite friendly. I think they could tell I was new to the college, because most of them smiled at me and some asked my name and where I had come from.

I can't believe how big the college grounds are. It covers over two square miles of prime real estate, in the middle of the Achimota forest reserve. There are buildings for studying, a library, museum, printing press, cadet square, two chapels, three dining halls, two gymnasia, a post office, extensive sports playing fields, swimming pool, cricket, oval, basketball, tennis and squash courts, botanical gardens, a model village for college employees and residential blocks. A short distance from the school's central campus we come across a golf course, a police station, a staff village for the school's non-teaching staff, a large farm and a hospital.

We learn that after the First World War, the Governor of the then Gold Coast, Sir Frederick Gordon Guggisberg, established the college as part of his plan to reform the country's educational system. Many notable Africans have emerged from the college, including heads of state (Dr Kwame Nkrumah, John Evans, Atta Mills, John Dramani Mahama), politicians, academics, scientists, doctors, lawyers, engineers and educators. The school's founding doctrine has been to enable its graduates 'to know the life that is life indeed and go forth from it as living waters to a thirsty land'.

After the tour I thank the prefect and walk with Kwame to the main road. It breaks my heart that he will be returning home. If only he could stay a little longer, but then he would miss the bus and my parents would stay up all night worrying. He must have read my mind, because he turns to me with sad eyes and throws his arms around me.

'Kofi, be good boy. I go back home, but I come again very soon.'

He must have seen the tears in my eyes, because he holds me tighter and pats me on the back.

'Thank you for coming,' I say, trying not to cry.

'I hate to leave, but can't miss bus' he says. 'Promise you be good. Stay away from bad boys and study very, very hard.'

'I promise.'

'And if anyone bothers you, I come back and break every bone in their body.'

That makes me laugh. I know he will, but I pray to God that he doesn't have to.

'I will be fine.'

'Good. Keep smiring.'

He gives me another hug and nearly crushes my bones. Then he sees a taxi, stops it, jumps in and waves. I wave back with all my strength. My hand continues to turn in the air as the taxi speeds away. I can't stop the tears.

I remember how composed Maame was until I got on the bus bound for Accra. Just before the bus pulled away she broke down and had to be consoled by Papa. I was sad then, but I didn't really get how she felt until now. I don't know how I will cope without her beautiful smile, laughter, soothing voice and mouthwatering dishes.

Later that night, as I try to sleep, the lecture I had from Papa echoes in my head. 'My dearest son, remember where you come from and don't ever forget how much we adore you. Respect your teachers and your elders, obey the school rules, and avoid any kind of trouble or temptation. Most importantly, no distractions. Concentrate solely on the reason why you are at college - your education!'

Chapter Seven

Gazing out of the window from my second floor dormitory, I watch the stars in the clouds. It has been a month since I left home. The first few weeks were scary and lonesome. I have grown up very fast and learned so much – rules, routines, names, faces, buildings and interesting subjects and things I had never done, like learning to play the piano. The food is OK but no match for Maame's cooking. I have made a lot of friends and have two best friends, Nii Adjetey from Osu and Chukwudimma from Nigeria. I call them Nii and Chuks. We have so much in common – football, tennis, music, poetry and food.

Nii's father left home when he was a toddler and he was brought up by his mother. She sells kenkey and fish at the Kenkey Supermarket in Osu.

Chuks has twelve brothers, eight sisters and four stepmothers. His father is a governor in Abuja and his mother lives in London. Although his father has many houses around the world, a private jet, yacht, luxury cars, butlers, chefs, maids and security guards, he is humble, down to earth and hilarious.

Some of my friends are very happy to be here. It's the only way they can have a decent meal. They had to work really hard, day and night, to get a scholarship here. Others come from homes that are worse than prison. Hearing what they have been through - the endless chores, beatings and insults - makes me realise how fortunate I am. It seems physical, emotional and sexual abuse happen to children all over the world. It doesn't matter how rich or poor they are, gender, colour, intellect or social status. The stories of battling parents, infidelity and divorce open my mind to things I never thought of.

Unlike some of my classmates, who never study but always do well, and those who leave it till the last minute, learn the text off by heart and *chew and pour*, I need to pay attention in class and go over what is taught several times before I get it. Sometimes when I am struggling to understand what we have been taught I tell the teacher after the lesson. Most of the teachers are really good. They will make time to go over what I failed to understand.

All except Mr Stone, my maths teacher. The first time he introduced himself to the class, he left us with a lasting impression of fear. I have never seen him smile. He expects us to understand everything he teaches and anyone who gets below 80 percent has to stay on after school and do two hours of revision.

I like to look smart - clothes washed and ironed, shoes polished, hair neatly combed. It makes me feel good. I didn't expect to win a prize for being the best-dressed boy in my year. Soon after that I started getting lots of compliments, mostly from senior girls and female teachers. They would say, 'Damn, you are just too fine!' or 'Isn't he cute?' or 'You have style and manners, keep it up'.

Sometimes it feels good and other times I get shy and embarrassed. I always say 'Thank you!' but I don't let it go to my head. Even though I appear to be outgoing and have lots of friends, I still miss my family.

Chapter Eight

Her beautiful face is glistening from the harsh rays of the sun. She draws closer, devouring me with her eyes. The corners of my lips switch into a smile. I can feel her breath on my face. She kisses me. I kiss her back, on the lips. Then I smell her sweet perfume - lavender and roses - and know it has to be Tamara. She takes my hand and leads the way. Bare arms, caramel and smooth like velvet. I follow her voluptuous body, which is swaying like a pendulum. It's like I am up in the clouds, looking down on the oceans, hills and valleys. I think am about to explode.

Suddenly I wake up. It's just a dream. Damn! I am in a dormitory full of boys, some snoring and others mumbling in their sleep. The heat is unbearable. It's dark outside. Oh, the stench! It is so strong, I am sure someone has let off a stinking fart. I turn to my side and pull the bedcovers over my head. I am sweating all over. But that's not all. It's happened again. Another sticky patch. Damn! I had forgotten all about Samira.

I make my way to the bathroom. Then I turn on the light, open the window and do what I should have done several weeks ago.

Dear Samira,

I hope you are well.

Our last day together has never left my mind.

There is so much more I wanted to say,

but time was not on our side.

I like you more than you will ever know.

I wish you were here with me.

Be forever mine.

Kofi

I fold the letter and seal it in an envelope. Then I turn off the light and go back to sleep.

As soon as I finish breakfast I head to the library. It's a beautiful Saturday morning, but with three lots of homework, I doubt if I will see the sun.

Shortly after noon I tuck Samira's letter into my breast pocket and head to the post office.

'Kofi!"

I don't need to turn around. I know that voice. It's Nii. He's with Chuks.

'Where have you been?' he asks as he reaches me. 'We've been looking everywhere for you!'

'We are not joined at the hip, you know.'

'Oooooh! Someone seems to have woken up on the wrong side of the bed.' Chuks sniggers. 'Is his Lordship mad at us?'

'Of course not! I had to finish Mr Stone's endless equations. That man thrives on seeing us suffer. I need to clear my head and post this.' I take the letter out of my pocket.

'Can I come?' Chuks asks.

'Of course!'

'I am coming too, and I don't need your permission.' Nii kisses his teeth. 'Your Lordship my foot!'

'Who have you written to?' Chuks asks, stretching his neck to look at the letter.

'A friend.'

'Kofi has a girlfriend! Kofi has a girlfriend!' they chant. I ignore them.

'What is she like?' Nii asks.

'Very pretty and smart.'

'Oooooh! How old is she?' He continues.

'Twelve.'

'What do her parents do?' Chuks asks.

I take a deep breath. 'Why are you so inquisitive? Her father is a lawyer and her mother is a midwife.'

'Have you done it?' Nii asks excitedly.

'Done what?' Sometimes I can't believe what comes out of his mouth.

'Kofi is a virgin!' he laughs.

'Aren't you?'

'Me?' He asks, chest puffed out. 'I did *it* a long time ago.'

'How could you have done *it* a long time ago?' I enquire. 'You are only thirteen.'

'So what?' He replies. 'Everyone I know has done *it*.'

'You know me, and I haven't. Are you telling us the truth?' Chuks asks.

'Are you calling me a liar?' Nii frowns.

'Sorryooo, I beg,' Chuks pleads.

Nii adjusts his collar and grins cheekily. 'The first time was with Larteyley, my next-door neighbour. That was three years ago.'

'You did it when you were *ten*?' Chuks asks, eyes wide open.

'Yeah! I had done lots of touching before that, but not the full thing.'

'OK, carry on.' I say. There is no doubt that he started young.

'*Charley*,' he continues, 'the girl had been begging for it for a long time, taunting me with her hot pants and batty riders. At first I didn't know what to do, but my friends said it was easy. Anyway, she came to my house one evening, knowing very well that my mother would be at the night market. The minute she started shaking her tits in my face and calling me a *mummy's boy*, I knew I had to give it to her. I kissed her. She kissed me back and started touching me. I got excited. Before I knew it, *it* was all over.'

'*Chineke meeeeeeee!*' (Oh my God)' cries Chuks. 'Ghana boys. You go kill me!'

'Stop that nonsense!' shouts Nii. 'Nigerian boys do worse than that. Don't act like you have never been with a girl before!'

'Noooo, I beg. My name, Chukwudimma, means God is good. He is the reason I am here today and for that reason I will never try any form of temptation, abomination or fornication. *Tufiakwa!* God forbid!'

'Are you sure?' I ask Chuks. He seems so worldly.

'Aaaa! I am very very sure. You see oooo. It is not that I have not been tempted. Many girls and women have tried. Even when I say never, they still try to find my weak moment. I have had it from all directions, but they will never get me. *Chai!* The devil is a liar! Some of the mothers are Satan in disguise. They think because my father is rich they can trap me with their daughters and enrich themselves. They bring gifts and all sorts of food. Some have even tried juju, just to make me like their daughters. But my faith is stronger. Any evil thought or deed is automatically reversed - back to sender!'

'Are you telling me that you have never felt attracted to a girl?' Nii queries doubtfully.

'Ehhhh, as for attraction, I feel it all the time. Some of the girls are too beautiful, even here. So I talk to them, flirt a little and hold hands. That is all. Any more and I know I will cross the line, so I find a way to move myself out of the situation. Girls can be dangerous, and I don't like playing with fire.'

'My dear friends,' I say as we reach the post office, 'one should never rub bottoms with a porcupine.'

Chapter Nine

It's our third year at college. Chuks used to be the shortest, but at six foot he is almost as tall as me. Nii has grown about three inches and is nearly five foot nine inches. He has grown bigger too. At nearly fourteen stone he is over four stone heavier than me and Chuks.

It's Sunday, so we meet at the tennis court after church and play for about an hour. Shortly after lunch we fetch our books and head to the library. After studying for over four hours I am starving. I don't know if I can last the full hour before dinner. As it's nearing the end of term our chop-boxes are severely depleted.

Clutching our books, we tread lazily along the tree-lined Avenue. I focus on the beautiful sunflowers and take in long gulps of fresh air, hoping it will quench my hunger.

Nii and Chuks are checking out a group of pretty girls when a junior boy runs towards us.

'Good afternoon,' he says to us and turns to Nii. 'You have a visitor. Your mother is in reception.'

Nii's face lights up like the morning star. He throws his books at us. With a new boost of energy he sprints to the reception block. We follow closely behind.

Seeing Nii cradling in his mother's arms makes me wonder what has become of the big man who seems to know everything.

'Mmaa, meet Kofi and Chuks,' he says with a big smile.

I reach out my hand to greet her, but she ignores it and throws her ample arms around me. I look helplessly at Chuks as she smothers me with love. Even though she only comes up to my chest, she feels as strong as an ox. I try to keep a straight face when she sucks the air out of Chuks. He exhales when she releases him.

'I hear so much about you,' she says with a broad smile. 'You are like brothers to Nii Adjetey, so you are all my children. I bring you a little something. Be good and continue to look after each other.'

We nod obediently and thank her.

After a long chat in Ga, Nii walks her to her car and

returns with a huge basket. He looks miserable, but not for long.

The flavours drifting out of the basket make my stomach rumble. I can't wait to examine what is beneath the white napkin. Nii seems to be struggling with the basket. If I wasn't carrying my books and half of his, I would grab it from him and gallop to the dormitory.

The room is empty when we arrive. Throwing the books on Nii's bed, we wash our hands, crash onto the concrete floor and dive into the basket.

Beginning with the starter - yam, turkey tail, *shito* (chili and prawn sauce) and *kelewele* (fried plantain) - we move swiftly on to the main course, jolof rice and chicken. We haven't even touched the Kenkey and fish, banku and okro soup or chocolate cakes and yet my stomach is bulging.

Nii is dripping with sweat as he sucks marrow out of a bone and licks his fingers. Chuks continues to wipe his nose with the back of his hand. He loves spicy food, but his body just can't take it.

'Nii, your mother is something else' he sniffs. 'This is the best food I have ever tasted.'

'This is very good' I say, licking my fingers. 'You should come and spend the weekend with me when we break up. My mother makes the most delicious fufu and palm-nut soup.'

'I will,' says Chuks.

'And me,' Nii adds. 'I would love to meet your girlfriend too.'

The bell rings for dinner. We glance at each other. Even without words, we each know instantly what the others are thinking. Up until now we have tried our best to obey the school rules. The prospect of falling out of line brings back memories of primary school, where any sign of insolence resulted in long harsh strokes administered with such fury that the flesh stung for weeks. Luckily I was spared from any of the whippings. Here though, it's more likely to be a detention.

I look around. My friends are sprawled on the concrete floor. They look like they could be dozing off any minute and I can barely move. As I flop back on the floor, I pray that our indiscretion never comes to light.

Chapter Ten

I gained admission to the University of Science and Technology in September 2012 and am very close to fulfilling my dream of becoming a doctor. Everyone in my family is delighted, especially Grandpa and Maame.

Kwaku has stepped into Papa's shoes. He is studying agriculture science. Papa is over the moon. It has taken the pressure off me. He will be a great cocoa farmer.

Samira is in her last year at Wesley Girls' College. She plans to study law. We still write to each other and meet during school holidays.

The last time we met, we went for a stroll along the Pumpum river. It was a beautiful sunny day. When we got to the Kintampo waterfalls I took her hand and kissed it. She said 'Kofi, your voice is much deeper and I love your Adam's apple, it's cute.'

'You have changed too,' I said.

'How?' she asked excitedly.

'You have grown a lot taller, your bust is bigger and your hips are wider. It makes you more womanly, more elegant and beautiful.'

'Really?' she asked, big brown eyes looking into mine.

'Yes, and you have now been my girlfriend for eight years.'

'Wow, you remembered!'

'And when I finish medical school, I would like to make you my wife.'

She blushed. Then she kissed me, on the lips.

ND - #0526 - 270225 - C0 - 203/127/5 - PB - 9781861514332 - Matt Lamination